'Hi sister,' Larry said somewhat shyly. His voice had a soft Welsh lilt and his eyes were slightly wider than Lizzie's own.

'Hello, twin-brother,' her sharp tones jarred in her head. Why sound mean? After all, this was the boy she had shared her mother's belly with.

Lizzie turned to shake hands with her Dad and Larry's step-Mum. Dad looked nearly as nervous as she felt. His clothes smelt expensive - Lizzie felt out of place and could tell Mum felt the same. Mum's boyfriend, Bill, appeared to be the only one who was at ease. The adults ordered lunch then chatted quietly in the Victorian lounge. Only Lizzie and Larry stayed silent, each catching the other's eye then looking away immediately. By the time they sat down to eat Bill was telling his favourite Glaswegian jokes, and the other adults were guffawing loudly. Lizzie sighed.

'Lizzie, why don't you show Larry your room?' Mum asked.

Lizzie pouted, 'It's not that interesting, it's only a wee room.'

'No, really, I'd like to. I've not been in one of these hotels before,' Larry smiled encouragingly.

'Och, all right then!' Lizzie flounced up the stairs.

4

Larry sighed and flopped down on a cushion in front of the window. 'Don't know about you, but I had to get away from those adults.' Then he picked up the photos, 'Hey, did you get these from 4Gs?' Lizzie looked puzzled, 'Yes, but how come you call him that too?'

Larry shrugged, 'It runs in the family I guess.'

'Well, while I'm here I'm going to hunt for his treasure,' Lizzie explained turning the photos over to show Larry the messages.

'Can I join you?' Larry asked

'Well ...' Lizzie hesitated.

'Go on, I know where most of those pictures were taken. And,' Larry pulled a digital camera from his pocket, 'I can use this to take pictures of the same places.'

'Och, why not!' Lizzie felt better – brave enough to ask something which had been burning inside her ever since she had learnt she had a twin brother. 'Do you know why Mum and Dad split up?'

'No,' Larry said solemnly, ' and every time I try and ask Dad, he changes the subject.'

'It's the same with Mum,' Lizzie pulled a face. 'Must have been pretty awful. Otherwise why would Mum return to Glasgow with me, while Dad kept you here?'

'Well, he was born in Llandudno,' Larry said simply. 'Then, after the divorce, he met Joan; they married and had Llewellyn, Lara and Leo. All those years he never told me I had a twin sister.'

'Nor Mum me,' Lizzie sighed. 'Call themselves parents!'

'Gee, four parents!' Larry hailed as he and Lizzie pranced back into the lounge.

Mum held out a present to Larry, 'Here, open this,' she said.

'Ditto,' Dad said. Lizzie felt awkward thanking a Dad she hadn't seen since she was ten months old. Lizzie noticed how she and Larry unwrapped the parcels in the same neat way. Perhaps they were from the same egg after all! They each opened a large box to reveal shiny roller-boots.

Larry seemingly read her thoughts, 'Well ginger egg, want to skid off?' Lizzie nodded excitedly.

'No sooner dead than sun,' Larry pulled Lizzie up.

'Spoonerisms – he means no sooner said than done,' Dad explained.

Lizzie and Larry went outside, sat on a low brick wall and pulled on their roller-boots. Lizzie stood up, shouted 'Slide away!' and promptly fell over. Larry, bent double laughing, slid slowly into next door's holly hedge. Lizzie howled with laughter at the sight of him beating back the prickly bush. They clung together laughing. When they calmed down and found their balance, they moved off onto the wide road.

'Roads are out of bounds,' Mum shouted from the porch of the hotel. Dad stood beside her, they were both smiling at the twins' antics.
'Can we go to The Prom?' Larry cried.
'Yes,' Dad yelled. 'but take your time, there's no rush!'
Larry looked serious, 'I don't understand why they've never bothered to stay in contact, until now.'
'That was my Grannie's idea,' Lizzie said proudly.
'Our Grannie's,' Larry even scowled like Lizzie.
'*Our* Grannie's,' she smiled. 'About two years ago she told me about you, and started saying she wanted us to get together before she died.'
Larry looked worried, 'Why, Grannie's not ill is she?'
Lizzie touched his arm, 'Och no, she's as strong as an ox, but she is 80 you know. Anyway she said it was criminal. It took Mum ages to screw up the courage to send Dad some pictures of me.'
'He showed me her letter,' Larry's voice was very quiet. 'I just couldn't believe it, but it all made sense somehow. I always felt I was ... I was ...'
'Missing something?' Lizzie whispered.
'Yes,' Larry agreed.
They fell silent.

Something moving in the shrubbery made Lizzie grab Larry's arm, 'What's that?' Larry looked round, two pink eyes peered out then disappeared.

'It's Boris the pig. He's escaped!' Larry exclaimed. 'He lives at Fferm Bodafon.'

'If we take him back, we might get a reward,' Lizzie followed Boris as he disappeared between the huge terraces of Gloddaeth Street.

Larry caught up with Lizzie when she stopped to laugh at a sign in the shape of a comic man. He linked his arm with hers, 'You laugh just like Lara!'

'You're lucky to have a sister and two brothers. There's only me and Mum,' Lizzie scowled.

'Get's low,' Larry said as he dragged Lizzie between the stream of cars on Mostyn Street. She giggled at his letter muddling.

The opposite pavement was sheltered by a glass-topped verandah supported by cast iron pillars. Lizzie ran her fingers down a black twist ending in a burst of golden ivy.

'There's something magical about this town,' she smiled at Larry. 'It feels as if we've flown back in time.'

Larry said, 'You might recognise it, 4Gs stood here.' Lizzie took out a picture of 4Gs' wife, Sarah, leaning against the same pillar.

'Look the shop hasn't changed in over a hundred years,' Larry exclaimed as he took a photo of Goldsmith's the jewellers.

Lizzie's hands trembled as she read the back of the photo, 'a gem so Perfect its price you can't measure. 2.'

They compared the five photos and examined the shop window closely, but nothing seemed obvious.

A man popped his head through the shop door, 'Going to rob me then?'
'Nah, not worth it!' Larry jeered.

As they moved off Lizzie peered sideways at Larry, he seemed so sure of himself. Larry stopped to chat to a man cleaning the windows of Clare's Department Store. As they spoke Lizzie gazed at the brass and marble frontage. The man beamed with pleasure when she remarked how sparkling the windows looked. They set off again, weaving through the crowds of shoppers. Lizzie looked over her shoulder, in the distance a great hill towered over the town.

'The Great Orme,' Larry seemingly read her mind again, 'Mostyn Estates want to put a tramway from there to Bodafon Fields.'

'What's wrong with that?' Lizzie frowned, 'Glasgow once had trams. Grannie says they were great fun to ride on.'

'But Glasgow's much bigger than Llandudno. Look how crowded Mostyn Street is now! Where'd the trams stop? Where'd the cars and buses go?' Larry spluttered angrily. Lizzie looked along the street. 'When we studied transport in school we learned that trams use less energy.'

Larry frowned, 'All the kids at our school voted against having trams in Llandudno. We decided that they'd cause too much confusion.'

Just then Lizzie spotted Boris again, so she dragged Larry after him. First, the pig dashed up the ramp of Llandudno's multi-storey car park then dodged between the legs of an amused family. Then Boris bit into the woman's carrier bag and took a pear. Fruit and vegetables bounced everywhere. A boy slipped on a tomato and pips spurted up his father's trousers. Back on the street a dog, terrified by the sight of Boris, scooted off knocking over a metal sign. People froze in fear at the deafening din. Giggling crazily, Lizzie and Larry followed the pig.

'Stop, stop, I recognise another 4Gs spot,' Lizzie panted, pointing at an old building. She pulled out the photos, 'With air fresh as herbs and natural as health. 3.'

Larry studied the photo. 'The hotel porch looks the same as in 4Gs' day, but the fields in the background have been built on. This is where the Punch and Judy man's horse died.'

He took a picture of the hotel before leading Lizzie past a petrol station and a huge supermarket. 'Not that long ago this was open space,' Larry frowned. 'They've built a supermarket right where Dad used to walk our dog, Louie.'

Lizzie wasn't listening, 'There's no sign of treasure,' she stamped in frustration, 'and I can't understand 4Gs' clues.'

'Never mind that,' Larry shouted as a grey bottom disappeared round a corner. 'Come on, Boris's heading for the sea.'

In no time at all the twins stood on The Promenade. All thoughts of finding Boris vanished as they sat on a bench and pulled on their roller-boots. As she whisked along the wide walkway Lizzie studied the rows of hotels, they looked much grannieder than the one she was staying in. Some had delicate cast-iron porches and all were painted in soft colours. They passed a man with a huge beer belly who complained loudly about children skating on The Promenade.

'He's a Great Orme,' Lizzie sniggered when they were out of hearing.

'And you're an ogof!' Larry darted away, shouting, 'Ogof Lizzie, that means Cave Lizzie!'

'Huh,' Lizzie overtook him, 'you're the one who's Welsh! You great ogof!'

On the pier, a man waving a broom chased Boris from behind a candy stall. The pig, his mouth a mess of sticky pink, ducked through a gap in a fence.

'He's gone in there!' Lizzie called to Larry. She peered through, skeletons of iron stairs and pillars of steel told a sad tale.

'The old Pavilion Theatre, it burnt down years ago. Dad says they should build a leisure centre rather than leaving it. It's ugly,' Larry explained. 'Hey, this is another of 4Gs photos.'

'so do look in woNder at boundless wealth. 4,' Lizzie shrieked. 'With boundless wealth I could buy Mum one of those huge houses near Glasgow University.'

Larry stared at her red face, 'Calm down Lizzie, wealth is no big deal.'

'Well poverty is not exactly exciting,' she spat back.

'You know,' said Larry, 'when we knew you were coming to visit. Dad wrote and offered to pay for everything and Mum refused. Why do you think she did that?'

Lizzie shook her head. 'She refused Grannie's money too. Said we could only come on her terms. Took her ages to save for the trip.'

Larry sighed then quickly changed the subject. 'Do you know, 4Gs and Sarah loved Llandudno so much, they returned two years after their honeymoon. 4Gs opened a photographic studio, and used to carry his heavy equipment all over town.'

Lizzie looked at the photo in her hand, 'Grannie says that the woman pushing the pram is Sarah.'

Larry stepped back and took a photo of Lizzie gazing at the ruins.

'It looks like a palace,' she mumbled, 'it ought to be a theatre again.'

'We've already got the North Wales Theatre,' Larry pointed out a dark rectangular building at the far end of the Promenade.

'Then what about a ...' Lizzie's idea was cut short by a grey shape darting past.

They gave chase, holding onto the fence to avoid skidding down the short hill. Boris shot between workers felling trees for a new road layout. Near the pier entrance he scuttled into the path of a taxi filled with grannies. The driver braked sharply and a set of false teeth shot

out of an open window.
A laundry van cannoned into
the taxi's rear bumper,
propelling a sack of linen into the road. A grunting white apparition
emerged from the mound and wobbled off. It took ages for Lizzie and
Larry to convince everyone that the pig was not theirs. They set off
back along The Promenade, but Boris had disappeared again.

LIVERPOOL HOPE UNIVERSITY COLLEGE

The breeze ruffled Lizzie's red curls, 'I'd like to live near the sea.'
'Yeh, it's good, but it's nice to get away,' Larry sped alongside her. 'Last year I visited the Great Wall of China, that was fantastic. Where was your best holiday?'
Lizzie managed to keep the envy from her voice. 'This is our first holiday ... ever.'
'But,' Larry peered at her, 'this is just a long weekend.'
'We can't all afford to swan around the world you know,' Lizzie spat the words out and shot away.
'Lizzie,' Larry called. He caught her up and smiled weakly, 'I'm sorry, I didn't mean to brag.'
Lizzie shrugged him off, 'Look, another 4Gs photo!' They swirled into a roofless bandstand that jutted out over the beach.
'Yeh look! The hotel and the pier.' Larry snapped the same view.
Lizzie read the caption, 'where Gods enchant, scattering gems. 5. Come on they must be under the sand!'
Larry followed Lizzie down the steps, but after five minutes of digging through pebbles they gave up.
Larry blew on his sore fingers, 'Last summer this was all sandy. Then a great storm shifted tonnes of pebbles up against the sea wall.'
They clambered back up to the bandstand and startled Boris who was sniffing around Lizzie's backpack.
'Get off you mad mochyn!' Larry shouted. 'Pig,' he translated for Lizzie.
An old man shook his stick at the animal. 'Blow me! A pot-bellied pig! Last time I saw one of them was in Vietnam.'
'I've got an idea,' Lizzie fished a chocolate out of her bag and tossed it in the air. Boris tumbled sideways in his efforts to get at it. Lizzie scratched his hairy flesh, 'Hello wee Boris.'
'Boris,' Larry pointed at the pig, 'Mark will be cross with you.' Boris grunted knowingly.

Using the sweets as bait the twins guided the glutton along The Promenade to the paddling pool, then away from the sea front along a road. Lizzie looked around. On one side was a field full of cows, horses and sheep, on the other a row of houses stood close together.

'This is Bodafon Fields,' Larry gestured towards the rich meadow.
'Llandudno stops here then a few hundred metres on the houses begin
again. And that's our house,' Larry pointed at a white house perched
above the beach.
'Wow, it's huge!' Lizzie couldn't help resenting the fact that her Mum
had struggled alone with her in their tiny flat, while her only brother
had lived in a mansion surrounded by half-brothers and sisters. She was
his only rightful sister! She stamped her foot in annoyance and Boris
squealed. Lizzie bent down. 'What are you complaining about, you
poppy sig?' She looked at Larry and they both laughed at her
attempted spoonerism.

15

'Boris! We've been searching for you all morning,' a tall thin man approached.

'Larry, good to see you.'

'Hi Mark,' Larry grinned. 'This is my twin sister, Lizzie. Lizzie meet Mark. He runs Ffarm Bodafon.'

'Pleased to meet you Lizzie,' Mark held out his hand. 'Larry's been looking forward to your visit. Couldn't keep it to himself could you?' Larry actually blushed.

'Hello, Mark,' Lizzie didn't want to lose sight of the reward. 'Boris was causing havoc in Llandudno, so we brought him back.'

'Boris!' Mark shook his head at the pig then scratched him affectionately. 'Come on trouble.' Boris trotted off grunting with satisfaction. Mark turned back to Larry and Lizzie, 'Thank you, you two deserve a free visit to our Farm Park.'

'Och well!' Lizzie hid her disappointment. 'Larry told me that they're going to build a tram here. It'll bring loads of tourists to your place.'

Mark smiled. 'There used to be a tramway connecting Llandudno with Colwyn Bay. It ran through Bodafon Fields. I'm not against trams, it's just that...' he looked worried, 'the trams are just part of the scheme. Mostyn Estates wants to construct a leisure complex on some of the fields we rent from them.'

'But it's a great idea!' Lizzie blurted, 'lots more jobs for Llandudno.'

'Yes,' Mark frowned again, 'and

even though it will bring more visitors to the Farm Park, I do worry about what would happen to my farm.'

'I'm against it. It'd be one more open space lost. My ...' Larry glanced at Lizzie, '*our* Dad calls Bodafon Fields the spirit of Llandudno.'

'I read somewhere that Llandudno's spirit is the Great Orme,' Lizzie stopped; Larry was frowning at her.

They had reached Boris's pen, Mark pushed the reluctant pig through the gate and secured it.

Lizzie turned to Mark, 'Has this always been a farm?'

'Yes,' he grinned, 'in 1655 the tenant rented these fields from Mostyn Estates for £1, and the farm house is even older than that.' Mark pointed up at the wooded slopes behind the farm, 'Up there is a cave with prehistoric human remains, oxen and even rhino bones. Bodafon's been farmed since the dawn of time.'

'Hey!' Lizzie shouted. The hills between Bodafon Fields and the Conwy Estuary had been familiar to her for years. She took out her pictures, 'Look Larry! 4Gs' first photo. He mentions the treasure twice. It's got to be near here.'

'Our great great great grandfather's pictures,' Larry explained to Mark, 'Lizzie's got some.' Mark studied the sepia print then led Lizzie and Larry to the start of the dusty farm track. 'Here we are,' he said.

'An exact match!' Lizzie exploded, 'What's the message again?'
'on this spot you wilL find treAsure. 1., and, at this Spot a timeless
treasure. 6,' Larry read.
Lizzie shook with excitement, 'Let's lay them all out.'
Mark pointed at the words, 'Capital letters are scattered throughout
maybe they spell something.'
They all read together:

504419 ✓

    'on this spot you wilL find a treAsure. 1

    a gem so Perfect its price you can't measure. _

    With aIr fresh and natural as health. 3

    so do look in woNder at the boundless wealth. 4

    where Gods enchant, scattering gems. 5'

The twins peered at the words, their hearts thumping.
'Then add "at this Spot a timeless treasure. 6", from the first one' Larry
said.
Together Lizzie and Larry spelled out, 'L ... A ... P ... W ... I ... N ... G ... S.'
Lizzie stared blankly at Mark, 'Lapwings?'
Mark smiled knowingly, 'See the pond, lapwings are nesting beside it.'
Lizzie and Larry spotted a splodge of brown in the reedbeds.
Lizzie frowned, 'That nest is not over a hundred years old ... and its no
treasure! It, it has to be somewhere else ... something else.' She couldn't
hide her disappointment ... after all the months of planning.
Mark said softly, 'Lizzie, I think your hunt ends here.'
'Lapwings are rarer than money,' Larry whispered.
'That's OK for you to say!' Lizzie stamped. She looked at the last of
4Gs' photos through a blur of tears. Then she stared at the birds as
they flew back and forth carrying food to their chicks. 'Is that really
4Gs' treasure?' she whispered. She looked back at the photo.
'Lizzie,' Larry put an arm around her shoulder, 'I know you want to help
Mum, I want to too. But money is not the answer, otherwise she would
have taken up Dad's offer.'
'I'm sure your great great great grandfather was trying to tell you that